The Witch and the Holiday Club

It's the summer holidays and it's very hot. Simon and his friends, with his best friend, the witch, discover a smashing café where the ice cream is the best in town.

But Lady Fox-Custard does NOT approve! "It's absolutely *infested* with beetles, you know," she says to Simon's mother, and she decides to start a holiday club for "nice" children. As soon as the witch hears about the holiday club she wants one too. Suddenly the witch's sister, Tombola, arrives from Africa with all her pets. But the witch quickly gets fed up with snakes slithering all over the place and Tombola zooms off to camp in Lady Fox-Custard's garden! The summer holidays are far from dull.

The Witch and the Holiday Club is a special tie-in book with the second series about Simon and the Witch on BBC TV.

D0531184

The Witch and the Holiday Club

Margaret Stuart Barry

Illustrated by Linda Birch

YOUNG
LIONS

First published in Great Britain 1988
by William Collins Sons & Co. Ltd
Published in Young Lions 1988

Young Lions is an imprint of
the Children's Division, part of
the Collins Publishing Group
8 Grafton Street, London W1X 3LA

Printed in Great Britain
by William Collins Sons & Co. Ltd, Glasgow

Contents

Dedicated to
Emily May Bell

No more school. Never ever

"I am *never* going to go to school again!" said the witch. "Never ever."

George, the witch's long suffering cat, looked put out when he heard this. He was the sort of cat who liked to be on his own. When the witch was out, he could prowl around the house doing evil things. He could nose into cupboards and drawers and sniff at the witch's belongings. He could claw big holes in the hearthrug; snootch under the settee, and lick inside the pans. But most of all, he could crunch up the furniture when he was hungry. He got smacked of course, but he was well used to that, so it didn't matter.

The witch ignored George's sulky looks and rummaged out her school uniform. She hung it up on a coat hanger and examined it. It had porridge stains down the front of it; squirts of marmalade on the sleeves, and chewing gum on the back – there was

always lots of chewing gum on the school chairs. Also, most of the hem had come unstuck, but it was still far too good to throw away. The witch spat on her finger and tried to rub off some of the stains. Then she wrapped it up for Oxfam.

"Those Oxfam ladies will be mad keen to have it," she crowed.

Very pleased with herself, the witch started to do an Indian style war dance round the uniform, singing,

"Witches do not go to school,
That's me new fantastic rule."

The door burst open and Simon came in. Simon was the witch's very best friend.

"What on earth are you doing now?" he asked.

8

"What does it look like I'm doing?" snapped the witch. "I'm singing a song what I've just invented. I'm very clever at making up songs you see."

She sang it again, and waited for Simon to say what a brilliant song writer she was, and brilliant at everything else.

"That's stupid," said Simon. "And anyway, you'll have to go back to school next term."

"No I won't," said the witch. "I only went last term to learn how to read again. I can read my spell book now so that's that. School's for fluffy brained duffers."

"Oh well," Simon grinned. "Let's not talk about school now — it's the first day of the summer holiday. What shall we do?"

"Dunno," said the witch.

"We could go fishing," said Simon.

"It's too hot to go fishin'," said the witch. "I fancy doing something cold, like eating an ice cream. Or two or three, or maybe ten. I saw this smashing looking café the other day. It was called Valdini's."

"Let's go there then," agreed Simon.

The witch slammed on her hat and looked into the mirror to see if she was as beautiful as she remembered. Looking in the mirror meant swishing off a great deal of dust, some dead spiders, and the remains of a beetle which had mistakenly wandered into the path of the spiders. The witch peered at herself. Her eyes were pleasantly green, and still in the same place. Her nose was large and distinguished, and her hair was like grey wire wool – of the very best quality.

"Oh yes!" said the witch, admiringly.

"Ice cream," reminded Simon.

"Bucketsful," agreed the witch, wrenching herself away from the mirror.

They walked along together in the sunshine. Happy to be on holiday and chatting about how they were going to spend it. There were so many things one could do.

"Start a football team," suggested Simon.

"Paint the outside of the school purple," said the witch.

"Build a den at the bottom of my garden," said Simon.

"Build an ocean going liner," said the witch.

"You could be Batman and I could be Robin," said Simon.

"I could be the Queen of England, and you could be the Duke of Edinburgh," said the witch.

"You're getting silly now," said Simon.

"Here's Oxfam!" cried the witch. She went inside and plonked her uniform down on the counter.

"Just leave it there, Mrs . . . er," said one of the Oxfam ladies, not looking enormously interested.

The witch re-emerged, looking sulky.

"They were *terribly* pleased," she said to Simon.

"The one with the whispery voice and the watery eyes and the fat ankles was madly excited when she saw my uniform."

Simon, who had been looking through the window, grinned, and said nothing. They had wandered past the shops and were approaching rather a shabby part of the town. At the end of a row of dull looking buildings was a colourful looking café. It had 'Valdini's' written over the door. There were bright green tables and chairs, and checked tablecloths with matching curtains.

"This is it," said the witch.

Mr Valdini was wiping the counter and staring glumly round at his empty café. The coffee machine was hissing and puffing like a steam engine; cakes and biscuits were laid out under glass covers, and there was a delicious smell of hot spaghetti. At the other end of the counter was a glistening array of different coloured ice creams.

"This place looks great!" said Simon.

"I told you," said the witch, triumphantly.

Mr Valdini started to sniff and then he burst into tears.

"What's the matter with him?" asked Simon, embarrassed.

"What's the matter with you?" the witch asked Valdini.

"What's the matter with me?" asked Valdini, his

sobs turning into loud hiccups. "You are asking me, Mrs Tatty? Look at my café."

The witch had a good look all round, squinting and examining everything very closely.

"It's very nice," she said. "That's why I came here."

"Ees a beauuutiful café. Look how pretty the flowers, the onions, all very best plastic. Not one cheap stuff. And see this wonderful spaghetti," he stirred it mournfully with a spoon. "My Maria, she make it. How beeg and nice smelly the tomatoes."

"Oh I don't know – they're not all that smelly," said the witch, politely.

"And look at this ice cream," Valdini went on, "as

good as my grandpa used to make, and everybody would say, 'Papa Valdini make the best ice cream in Italy!' "

"That's what we came in for," said the witch, her tongue beginning to hang out, and wishing Valdini would hurry up and cheer up and give them some.

But Mr Valdini was still in the middle of wailing. "How many peoples do you see sitting in my café?" he went on.

The witch was getting bored looking round the café, but she had another quick look.

"Nobody," she said.

"You see nobodys too!" cried Valdini. "Business — ees so bad!"

"Is it?" said the witch, starting to sweat with the heat. "Well can we have ten ice creams please?"

"TEN!" gasped Valdini.

"To start with," said the witch.

Mr Valdini started to cheer up a little at that and rushed to serve them.

Simon and the witch chose a table near the window and started to eat their ice cream. They had chosen chocolate, vanilla, strawberry and banana, and the witch squelched them all together with her spoon and made loud icy sucking noises.

"We'll have ten more of those," she said, almost at once.

"This is a smashing place," said Simon. "It's a pity

more people don't come in here. Perhaps we could think of ideas to make them come."

"Perhaps we could," said the witch with a sniff, wiping chocolate ice cream off her mouth on to the back of her sleeve.

"What about going fishing now," said Simon.

"*Boring,*" said the witch. "Let's go back to your house for some lunch. I'm starving."

Simon's mother was hard at work as usual. She always looked a little hot and bothered. She looked even more hot and bothered when Simon arrived with the witch. She had only made enough scrambled egg for one. Simon sat down and tried to eat it, trailing his spoon through it listlessly.

"Have you been eating outside?" asked his mother.

"He's only eaten ten ice creams," interrupted the witch, eying Simon's scrambled egg hungrily.

"TEN!" gasped Simon's mother.

"Maybe it was eleven," added the witch. "I'll eat that, Mrs Woman. I love yellow yuck."

Without waiting for an answer, the witch sat down and gobbled up the eggs.

"I don't know how you could!" shuddered Simon, – "after all that ice cream!"

The witch wiped her mouth politely on the edge of the tablecloth.

"You ought to go to that café, Mrs Woman," she

said. "There aren't enough customers in it. Valdini was blubbering about it. He was crying all over the spaghetti and waterin' down the ice cream, and (the witch rescued a small piece of scrambled egg with her finger) . . . everything."

"Oh dear," said Simon's mother. "That does sound a shame. Poor man."

"We said we'd try and think of ideas to get people to go to his café," said Simon.

"Like free ice cream," muttered the witch, jabbing a wet finger at a toast crumb which had nearly escaped.

"Why don't you go and see Cuthbert?" Simon's mother suggested. "He might be able to think up something."

15

But Cuthbert was a prisoner in Horty Hall. His aunt, Lady Fox-Custard, was determined he was not going to spend his summer holiday just playing.

"You played around enough in the Christmas term," she was saying. "That pantomime was a disgrace!"

"The mayor liked it," mumbled Cuthbert.

"The mayor's a bumbling idiot!" snorted his aunt. "Ees got no refinement. He'd laugh like a drain if one was to slip on a banana skin."

Hopkins, the butler, who always stood like a bored stiff statue, smothered a giggle.

"I've got a book for you, Cuthbert," announced Lady Fox-Custard. "It's a lovely book. Expensive too. It's called *Little Problems are Fun*."

"But it's all about sums!" wailed Cuthbert in dismay.

"It is, after all, a holiday, Ma'am," interrupted Hopkins.

"Nobody asked you nothing!" snapped Lady Fox-Custard.

And she tottered across to the window table to finish her prawn salad, sighing heavily.

Simon and the witch arrived at the gates of Horty Hall and crunched up the drive.

"This place gives me the spooks!" whispered the witch. "Look at all them potty statues. They haven't even got clothes on!"

"Garden statues don't wear clothes," explained Simon.

"You'd think they'd wear more, not less," said the witch, and pulled the doorbell.

Hopkins opened the door.

"We've come to see his little Lordship," wheezed the witch, "Cutey Cuthbert."

Hopkins ushered them into the drawing room and said, "Master Simon and Mrs . . . er."

At once, Cuthbert cheered up. Lady Fox-Custard smiled wanly at Simon but scowled at the witch. The witch was a woman she definitely did not approve of. The woman was a trouble-maker and a bad influence.

"I'll sit down, shall I?" said the witch, collapsing heavily onto a fragile antique chair.

The chair made a cracking noise and tipped to one side.

"It's rubbish!" thought the witch to herself.

"We came to see Cuthbert," said Simon. "Can he come out to play?"

"*Play*!" boomed Lady Fox-Custard, a prawn trembling on the end of her fork. "Is that all you boys think about?"

The witch squinted viciously and pretended to look alarmed.

"Well, not exactly play," Simon struggled on, "more like writing. Writing down ideas and things."

"Writing, you say," said Lady Fox-Custard, stab-

bing another prawn. "Well I can't see no harm in that.
But don't be late, Cuthbert."

Cuthbert jumped up happily, and followed Simon
and the witch to the door. As they were leaving, the
witch waggled her wand slyly at one of the prawns
which changed into an enormous crab, became alive,
and started to crawl off the plate. They could hear
Lady Fox-Custard's screams as they ran off across the
garden.

The witch snatched up a begonia and pulled off the
petals as she ran. "She loves me, she loves me not, she
loves me, she HATES me," she giggled.

"You are dreadful!" Simon grinned.

"Sorry I haven't tidied up," apologised the witch

when they arrived at her house.

Simon looked stunned. The witch never tidied up.

"Sit down," the witch said. "Would you like fizzy worm juice or tea?"

"Tea," said both boys together.

"Right," said the witch, when she had made the drinks and sat herself down. "Now let's get on with the meeting. We are gathered here together . . ."

There was a knock at the door. Simon went to see who it was and found Jimmy standing on the doorstep. Jimmy blinked round the witch's kitchen to see if it was any worse than he had last remembered it. And it was.

"I'm bored!" he grumbled.

The witch humphed and carried on. "As I was

saying, we are gathered here together . . .''

"What for?'' asked Jimmy.

"Will you shut up, bird brain,'' snapped the witch. "You've made me forget now.'' She took off her hat and peered inside. Sometimes, the odd idea did escape inside there. But it was empty.

"We're trying to think up ideas to get customers to go to Valdini's café,'' explained Simon.

"Oh,'' mumbled Jimmy,'' still sulking at being called a bird brain.

"I know!'' cried Cuthbert. "Valdini could play loud Italian music.

"The Noise Stoppit Society'd complain,'' said the witch.

"We could help him to paint the outside of the café bright yellow and green,'' said Simon.

"That'd make people sick, instead of hungry,'' said the witch.

"We could help Mr Valdini with the cooking,'' suggested Jimmy.

"That's a really rotten idea!'' scoffed the witch. "It sounds like work. Everybody go away and think at home.''

Meanwhile, Cuthbert's aunt was getting very agitated. She looked at her watch and rang the bell for Hopkins.

"Cuthbert is very late, Hopkins.''

"It is only four o'clock,'' reminded Hopkins, "and

the summer holiday, Ma'am."

"Don't go on like a gramophone record!" snapped Lady Fox-Custard. "What you don't seem to realize is that my nephew isn't just some ordinary little boy. He's delicate. No doubt you were allowed to trollope around the streets until it was dark, but Cuthbert is very refined. Well, it's only natural, isn't it, with his parents being the Duke and Duchess of Do-Nuthin. You'd better go out and look for him before some coarse villain kidnaps him, or something."

"I can see his Lordship now," said Hopkins, huffily.

Cuthbert burst in, looking happy. He told his aunt about the meeting at the witch's house, and how they had all been thinking of ideas to get customers to go to Mr Valdini's café.

Lady Fox-Custard sniffed.

"I hope you don't mean that nasty, scruffy looking Italian café at the other end of town, do you?" she said. "I wouldn't like to see you going in there."

Cuthbert looked stricken. He wasn't sure whether his aunt had actually forbidden him to go into Valdini's or not.

Beetles and Spaghetti

The next day the witch was up early. She was sitting in the kitchen in her nightdress and curlers. George miaowed for some breakfast but the witch was far too busy to listen to him. George glared at her with ill disguised distaste. She looked like a large porcupine with the curlers sticking out round her head. He miaowed louder and rubbed his greasy fur across her legs as a further hint, but the witch went on with what she was doing. She heaved her heavy spell book onto the table and opened it with a slam. A cloud of dust rose up and poofed all round the room, causing George to have a fit of sneezing.

"Be quiet, for goodness sake!" scolded the witch. "I'm trying to find a special spell."

She ran a bony finger down the pages, muttering, ". . . how to save grotty Italian cafés from going broke. Pah!" she said at length. "This spell book's dead old fashioned. The world's overcrowded with rotten frogs and princesses!"

George shrugged his skinny black shoulders and started to nibble round the edges of a chair. A letter plopped through the letter box. It was a very boring letter. All it said was,

WANTED. OLD FURNITURE, PICTURES,
SILVERWARE. Etc.

"That's it!" hooted the witch. "I'll make adverts! Nobody will think of a better idea than that. I'll write one now. What a good job I'm so good at spelling. She stuck out her tongue carefully and wrote,

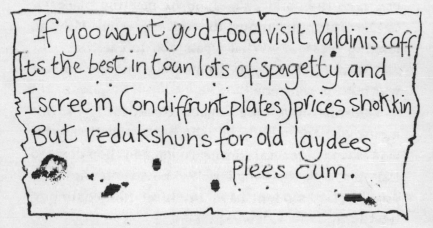

If yoo want gud food visit Valdinis caff Its the best in toun lots of spagetty and Iscreem (on diffrunt plates) prices shokkin But redukshuns for old laydees plees cum.

Pleased with the result, she waved her wand and a stack of adverts as high as the ceiling whizzed up.

"Heck!" gasped the witch, "How am I going to carry all those?"

Then her eye fell on a wheelbarrow and she filled it up with the adverts, ready to deliver, cackling at her cleverness.

Simon was sitting at his bedroom desk. He had just had exactly the same idea as the witch and was busily writing out adverts of his own.

"Nobody will think of a better idea than this," he was telling his mother. "We can pop an advert into every letterbox in town."

"I don't know," said his mother, doubtfully. "It's going to take you from now till Christmas."

Simon was undaunted.

Next day, Jimmy arrived at Valdini's café early. It was now the children's favourite meeting place.

"Beautiful mornings to you!" greeted Valdini, looking pleased. "What I gets you to eat?"

"Nothing, thank you," mumbled Jimmy. "I'm just waiting for someone."

Valdini's smile faded again. He fiddled with his moustache and wondered whether to tell Jimmy his café wasn't a general waiting room, and then decided that perhaps this small sickly boy with the large goggly glasses might have a rich relation coming to feed him.

At Horty Hall, Cuthbert was shifting around uncomfortably. He was waiting for his aunt to leave the room so that he could slip out to Valdini's. But Lady Fox-Custard seemed to be settled for the morning. She had given herself a present of an enormous box of chocolates and was busy sucking and crunching her way through them. In between crunches, she glanced at Cuthbert and frowned.

"A bored boy is a stupid boy," she said at length. "Why don't you get on with the book what I bought you?"

"I've finished it, Aunty. It was too easy."

"Too easy, eh? I think I'll go and exchange it for a harder one then," said his aunt.

"Oh yes, please," said Cuthbert, seeing his chance to be alone.

"Well, I must say that's more like it," Lady Fox-Custard beamed. She might have known a little genius like her nephew required difficult books to read. "Hopkins!" she bawled, "Bring my car round to the front."

As soon as Cuthbert was sure his aunt had driven away, he ran off towards Valdini's. He thought the other end of the town was really interesting. It was grey and dusty, but Valdini's café shone out like a beacon. The inside was even better. Cuthbert was enchanted.

"It's not common at all!" he said.

"Who do say it is?" cried Valdini.

"My aunt," said Cuthbert.

Valdini's face started to crumple, and his moustache began to droop.

"Please may I have some of your lovely spaghetti and a capuccino?" asked Cuthbert, hastily.

"Ahum!" coughed Jimmy.

"And some for my friend, please," added Cuthbert.

Valdini rushed off to tell his wife.

"Maria!" he shouted excitedly. "You hear that? A *customer*. With money." Suddenly doubtful, he zoomed back and peered over the counter. "You have got money, haven't you, sir?"

"Of course," said Cuthbert.

He liked Valdini. He was very funny. He reminded Cuthbert of a jumping firecracker. There was a commotion at the doorway. It was the witch arriving. She was struggling to squeeze her wheelbarrow through. A certain amount of paint was falling off the door. A lot in fact.

"Mama mia!" exclaimed Valdini." Ees thundering! The weather forecast she go wrong again."

"Oops!" said the witch. "It's only me. Either your doorway is too narrow, or my wheelbarrow's too wide. But don't worry. It's only an old wheelbarrow." Before Valdini could get cross, the witch asked for lemonade, and spaghetti with ice cream and bananas squished in the middle, and she showed him the adverts she had written.

"This is all my idea to save your café" she said, looking smug.

"The spelling, she's very comical," laughed Valdini, and then seeing the witch's smile shrink, added, "but it's a wonderful idea, you old tatty friend. You so kind to Valdini. I'm bigly touched."

"You can say *that* again," said the witch.

Then Simon came in with his neat pile of adverts.

"Snap!" cried the witch," — only I've got a hundred thousand more than you."

"Gosh!" said Simon when he saw the witch's full wheelbarrow. "And I sat up all night doing mine."

"I didn't," added Jimmy. "My bird brain wouldn't work."

"I wasn't allowed to sit up," grinned Cuthbert.

"Look! Another customer!" yelled Valdini.

The witch looked all round, and then under her chair.

"A pretty little girl looking in," said Valdini.

Sally had her face pressed to the window and was peering inside.

27

"Pretty! HER!" snorted the witch. "She's got a face like a squashed frog. She's got plaits like dead rats' tails. She's got a nose like a cracked ping pong ball. She's got a skin like a cold rice pudding."

"You not like her then?" asked Valdini.

Sally was coming in. "What on earth are you all doing in here?" she asked, nosily, peering round the café and pulling a face.

Nobody answered.

"I just happened to be passing," lied Sally. "I was on the way to the library. It's such a long holiday, I don't want to get behind with my reading."

"Of course not," said the witch. "You'd better go then."

But Sally was too curious to leave immediately so she sat down. She refused a drink, in case it had germs in it.

"She's not so pretty," muttered Valdini to his wife.

Jimmy told Sally about the witch's idea to advertise the café, and got his toes scrunched by the witch.

"This spaghetti's a bit boring," the witch remarked.

She rummaged in her handbag and produced a bottle of beetles.

Cuthbert's eyes bulged, fascinated and amused. But Jimmy glanced over nervously at Valdini.

"I don't think you're supposed to bring your own food into a café," he said. "I've seen notices about it.

It's a rule."

"Rules!" scoffed the witch. "I don't like rules. I never bother with them." And she scattered the beetles onto her plate. A few of them fell off the edge of the table and scuttled across the floor.

"Urrrrgh! Look!" screamed Sally. "There are beetles on the floor. I knew this was a dirty café. I'm going to report this to the Dirty Society!"

Valdini started to sob loudly. He was ruined, he was sure.

"She won't do anything," comforted the witch. "She's only a spiteful little kid." But Sally was scurrying away along the road, shocked, and smiling at once. Telling tales was one of her favourite things to do. By wonderful good luck, she bumped into Lady Fox-Custard who was just trying to reverse her Rolls

Royce out of the car park without hitting the same Mini twice.

Breathlessly, Sally told her about the dirty café, and the witch's plot to deliver adverts. "Cuthbert was there too," she added, gleefully.

"Surely not!" gasped Lady Fox-Custard. "How dreadfully disobedient of him! Oh, if only his parents hadn't been delayed on this second African expedition: hunting bugs and classifying them, or doing something awfully clever with them. It was such a trial being guardian to such an important boy — especially when he kept such bad company and was led by the nose into such *ghastly* places."

"Of course," said Sally. "We could write adverts about another café. A decent one. Then nobody would bother to go to Valdini's anymore."

Lady Fox-Custard eyed Sally with admiration. "That's brilliant," she said. "Perhaps you would like to write them out. I would myself, of course, but I have so many things to do. I have to open this terribly boring old hospital."

Sally ran off. She didn't bother to go to the library. She had something much better to do now.

As soon as Lady Fox-Custard arrived home, she swooped on the phone and rang Simon's mother. "I'm not one to interfere as you know," she treacled, "But I'm sure you'd like to know that your Simon was seen in Valdini's."

Simon's mother looked puzzled. "But it's quite a nice café, I thought," she said.

"Nice!" screeched Lady Fox-Custard. "It's a filthy place. It's absolutely *infested* with beetles you know. And at any rate, I don't think children should be spending their summer holiday in a café. Perhaps you could follow my example and get Simon some little puzzle books to occupy him."

"Er . . ." Simon's mother started to say, but Lady Fox-Custard had rung off.

"Who was that, Aunty?" asked Cuthbert as he came in.

"Just a business call," lied his aunt, delving into the second layer of her chocolates and sucking at them greedily. "By the way, I've got another book for you. It's called, *Hard Problems are Fun Too*."

"Thanks," muttered Cuthbert, going to hang up his jacket and sighing deeply.

Hopkins was half hidden behind the door. "Hey!" he whispered to Cuthbert. "Your rotten aunt's up to something. She's been on the phone to your mother, and she and that Sally girl are going to write adverts about some boring posh café. You'd better go and warn your friend, the witch."

"I'll do that," said Cuthbert. But his aunt would not allow him to go out again that day.

The witch, plus Simon and Jimmy, were planning which roads they were going to start delivering their adverts to.

"I put a load in the supermarket this morning," said the witch.

"That was good," said Simon.

"But that manager with the hooky nose and the big backside swep' 'em all up and put them in the bin."

The boys looked disappointed.

"But I got 'em out again," the witch continued, "and I stuck one on every loo roll. He'll never notice. He's proper gormless, that manager."

She poured out three glasses of water, pinged her wand at them, and turned them into something pink and fizzy. Refreshed, she shared out the adverts between them.

"I thought you had a lot more than this," said Simon, looking at his small handful. "Didn't you have a wheelbarrow full?"

A faint snore came from the direction of the wheelbarrow. George was stretched out asleep amongst a great pile of torn paper. He had words stuck to his whiskers. More words on his tummy. And a half chewed sentence sticking out of his mouth.

"That perishin' moggy!" screeched the witch. "He's gone and eaten them!"

Simon and Jimmy thought this was a good time to leave.

"I've got to go home first and get my running shoes," said Simon.

"Oh, I'm so glad I've caught you," said his mother.
"The new neighbours have just moved in next door.
The mother seems very nice, and they've got a *sweet*
little daughter called Angelica."

"Oh," grunted Simon, without much interest.

"Obviously," his mother went on, "she has no
friends yet, and she's about your age, so I've asked
her round for this afternoon."

Simon was aghast.

"But I can't stay in," he pleaded. "I've got a job to
do."

"Whatever it is, it can surely wait," said his
mother.

"But it can't, it can't," wailed Simon. "I've got to
post adverts for the witch. Immediately!"

"Oh, that," said his mother. "You'll have to do
them later. Anyway, I'm not sure it's a very good

idea. Lady Fox-Custard said you shouldn't be spending all your holiday in a café. She said I should buy you . . ."

Jimmy arrived, goggling impatiently.

"Aren't you ready?" he puffed.

"I'm not allowed to come out again," groaned Simon. "My mother's just gone and asked this girl round for tea. I've got to *play* with her!"

Jimmy was shocked.

"Play with a girl!" he gasped. "I'd better go and tell the witch."

"What a cheek!" snorted the witch. Her mouth set like a mouse trap and her green eyes turned several shades greener with jealousy.

Jimmy disappeared, hastily, and the witch rattled off with her wheelbarrow in the direction of Horty Hall. She squeezed as many adverts as she could through the letter box, and left, being careful to steer the wheelbarrow through as many of Lady Fox-Custard's prize begonias as she could manage. Pink heads and glossy leaves lay strewn around her. Cheered, she pushed on towards West Road, where Sally lived.

Meanwhile, Simon was shut up in his own house, waiting for the new neighbour to arrive. With a bit of luck, she might just be all right. But when Angelica rang the bell and Simon opened the door, he knew at once that he was in the middle of a tragedy.

Angelica, the Sugar Plum

Angelica stood on the doorstep, smiling more sweetly than a jar of honey. She was dressed in a brilliant white dress which flounced around her knees like a frothy wave. Her hair was angel blonde and was crowned with an enormous lemon bow. She had pink cheeks, and her blue eyes seemed to open wider and wider until Simon thought they might pop.

"Good afternoon, Simon," she greeted.

" 'lo," mumbled Simon, blushing.

"It's just *super* of you to invite me," Angelica went on. "My mummy is so pleased I've found a little friend already."

Simon looked even more aghast.

"And you're *much* better looking than my last boyfriend."

Simon looked desperately across at his mother. But she was just smiling. "Well, aren't you going to entertain your visitor, Simon?" she said.

Simon tried to pull himself together.

"We could go fishing," he spluttered.

But Angelica was horrified.

"What a *cruel* idea!" she gasped. "Those poor little fishies!"

So Simon trailed her up to his room and got out a box of soldiers.

"Soldiers!" exclaimed Angelica again. "Soldiers are so wicked! My goodness! They go marching around killing people."

She fluffed out the frills on her dress and smiled at Simon, sweetly.

"Actually," she went on, "my daddy is someone very high up in the army. But of course, he is terribly

careful not to shoot anyone. He goes to the Ministry of Defence in a lovely suit, and has ever such a nice umbrella. And he goes to lots and lots of super parties.''

She looked at Simon adoringly and added, ''You'd look absolutely dreamy in a nice suit.''

Bossily, she started to rummage around in Simon's playbox.

''Ah!'' she cried. ''Let's play Ludo. It's a fantastic game, especially if one cheats a tiny bit.''

Simon was amazed how often his counters toppled over, and how often Angelica threw a six which he didn't see. In the end, he decided it was much easier just to let Angelica cheat. Especially when she kept doing it anyway.

Mercifully, his mother called them down for tea and Angelica chattered on about the wonderful afternoon she'd had. Tomorrow she would bring her game of Trivial Pursuits.

''I can't read very well,'' she explained to Simon's mother, with another dazzling smile, ''and I only know the tiny, easy answers, but Simon could help me and that would be great fun.''

All the while, she kept gazing at Simon.

''I love the way your hair curls round your ears,'' she whispered.

With each new piece of conversation, she edged a little nearer to him, until to Simon's horror, she was nearly leaning on him.

"Anyway," Angelica chirped, "I'll *certainly* be coming again. Lots and lots of times."

And off she skipped.

"I don't believe it!" groaned Simon. "I'll get *ill* if she comes again. She's the worst person I've ever met."

"Honestly!" said his mother, "she does seem a tiny bit bossy perhaps, but she's not as bad as all that."

"She's worse, much much worse," mumbled Simon to himself as he trudged miserably down the road, not one of his adverts yet delivered. He started to run so that he could finish the job more quickly and get back to the witch's house, pushing two or three adverts into some letter boxes. At last the job was done and he raced back to see the witch.

The witch was sitting with her back to the door, looking lumpish, and she didn't turn round when Simon came in.

"I'm sorry I'm so late," he said. "I had this *dreadful* girl called Angelica to tea. I didn't ask her. It was my mother's idea."

The witch was sulking and continued to sit with her back to him. She started a long conversation with George, sweeping him off the floor and hugging him to her bosom. George looked astonished at this sudden display of affection and tried to spit. But the witch was clasping him too tightly.

"What a treasure you are," she cooed to him. "How lucky I am to have such a noble cat. Such a loyal cat. *You* wouldn't leave me for another would you? You wouldn't promise to do one thing and then skulk off to do something else."

George was struggling violently, and his claws were shooting in and out of his paws, trying to twist himself into a good scratching position. The witch had gone mad, he was sure. But the witch hung on grimly, keeping a sharp eye on George's dangerous claws.

There was a plop through the letterbox, and an advert fell onto the floor.

"Look at this!" cried Simon.

The witch was too nosy to keep up her sulks any longer and whizzed round. It was one of Lady Fox-Custard's adverts, advertising a delightful restaurant called the Claridge. It was a much smarter advert than Simon's or the witch's.

"Of all the cheek!" gasped the witch. "The interfering old baggage! The spiteful snooty lump of mouldy custard!"

Simon was delighted to see the witch back to her normal self.

"We could go round the houses and fish her adverts back out of the letterboxes," suggested the witch.

"But how would our arms reach?" asked Simon. "We could take my electric cleaner and *suck* 'em out!" she wheezed, triumphantly.

"Oh gosh!" said Simon. "Here we go!"

Only the witch could have thought of such an idea. Several passers-by stared at them as they pushed the end of the cleaner into each letterbox, but thought it must be some special kind of job the witch was doing, so took no notice.

"This is fun!" cackled the witch, making loud sucking noises as the adverts rattled up out of the letterboxes.

"Wait a minute," said Simon. "What's that white fluff sticking out of the end of the cleaner?"

Just then, a door shot open and a birdy little

woman shouted, "Hey you! What have you done with my cat?"

"Er . . ." spluttered the witch. "What cat?"

"My little Snowflake," bellowed the woman. "There . . . that's his tail sticking out of the end of your cleaner!"

"Oh, you mean *that* cat," gulped the witch. "We were just cleaning him. It's our job. We go round cleaning cats for people. We've just done yours free."

"Get him out of there at once," the birdy woman yelled, her face turning the most unusual shade of purple.

"All this fuss over a cat," the witch muttered to Simon.

41

She opened the cleaner and squeezed Snowflake out. The cat gave her a nasty look and shot into the arms of his mistress.

"But he's filthy!" screeched the woman. "He's covered in dust and bits of goodness knows what."

"But he hasn't got no fleas left on him," the witch said, and she wobbled away quickly.

"Honestly!" she said to Simon as soon as they were round the corner. "You just can't please some people!"

"Do you think we've done enough for today?" Simon said, nervously.

"We certainly have!" said the witch. "Especially when we just get shouted at by a mad looking woman. I think we deserve a drink."

Valdini was in a rare good mood. His café was quite full. He was mopping his brow and dashing around with trays full of food.

"Look how good business goes," he called to his wife, Maria, in the back. "So many customers! That kind, tatty woman done all this for us. I give her a big ice cream when she comes in – well, half price I give."

At that moment, Lady Fox-Custard's face appeared at the window. She was looking particularly peevish. She shaded her eyes and looked all round the café to see, if perhaps, Cuthbert was in there. She could not be too careful, she thought.

"I don't think that grand lady with the squashed cushion face likes Valdini's café Maria. Why she keep nosy nosy through the widow?"

Some real customers came in and he dashed back to work. Then Simon and the witch arrived.

"Ten banana, three vanilla, and twenty peppermint ices," ordered the witch, flopping down and fanning herself with the tablecloth.

All of a sudden, something large and dark flapped past the window.

"What on earth was that?" said Simon, startled.

"It look like a black thunder cloud to me," said Valdini, knowledgeably. "The weather forecast, 'ee go wrong again."

"I didn't think it looked like a cloud," said Simon, still alarmed. "It was something . . . strange and peculiar."

"Ha, you are a cooky little boy," laughed Valdini. "In Italy we have big fast thunders just like that."

But Simon was unconvinced, and even more so when he arrived home. The first thing his mother asked him was had he seen anything odd whilst he was out.

"It was like a whirlwind," she said. "Everything went dark for a few seconds. Whatever it was, it wasn't normal. All the dogs in the road started to bark at once. The cows in the distance were mooing, and soil blew up at the windows. You should have seen

43

the washing line next door. Angelica's dress was quite black."

"Spooky!" shivered Simon. "Perhaps there'll be something about it on the news."

But there wasn't. And he forgot about it.

Next day, Jimmy called for him bright and early and they set off towards the witch's house. As they approached her front door, they could hear deafening cackles, and wallops and thumps. Jimmy was terrified and tried to turn back, but Simon pulled him on. To one side of the door, lay a large, bulky lump of khaki material. Also, tossed around amongst the witch's cabbages and nasturtiums were a great many bashed looking boxes and canvas bags, tied together

with what appeared to be jungle vines. The boys were just starting to examine them when the door burst open and Tombola appeared. Tombola was the witch's sister and she came from Africa.

She was wearing a safari helmet with matching jacket and baggy shorts. She had about a hundred badges pinned all over her, and she carried her wand in a hip revolver case. Her face had been sunburnt a vivid purple colour, rather than the usual brown.

"Hey!" she shouted back at the witch. "You've got vandals in your front garden! Two crafty looking boys, up to no good by the looks of them."

The witch came out, and laughed. "That's Simon and his bird-brained friend," she explained. "You've

45

met them before. That time you came over with your gorrilla, Banana, and took him to school – you remember?"

"I go to so many places," said Tombola, with the air of someone very well travelled.

Jimmy was still keeping his distance, his hands pushed into his pockets to stop them shaking. But Simon was delighted to see Tombola.

"Where's Banana?" he asked, eagerly.

"Oh him!" snorted Tombola. "I haven't brought him. Couldn't. He's gone and got himself married."

"*Married!*" exclaimed Simon. "Who to?"

"Another gorrilla, of course," scoffed Tombola. "And I don't want to talk about it. The treacherous, ungrateful brute."

She went on to explain that it was partly because of Banana's unfeeling behaviour that she had come over for a holiday. Doctor Livingstone had recommended it.

"A short holiday, I expect?" put in the witch, who was already feeling a little fed up with her sister's visit.

"No, quite a long one, I thought," said Tombola. "Doctor Livingstone said I was suffering from Junglitis Nervosa."

"Humph!" snorted the witch. "That's nothing. I get Titchy House Nervosa, but I have to put up with it. Last term, I was suffering form Chronic Schoolitis, but I had to put up with that!"

Tombola just laughed, in a roaring sort of way.

"Never mind, old thing," she said. "We'll have a great time. Talking about titchy houses. I've brought my own accommodation this time. These two boys can help me to put it up, instead of just standing there looking gormless."

Simon and Jimmy struggled with the heap of khaki coloured material and it turned out to be a large messy-looking tent. Tombola got on with the job of sorting out her boxes.

"I've brought a few little pets," she told the witch, unpacking a writhing mass of snakes.

Jimmy went white with shock, and Simon was alarmed too.

Unaware of the panic she was causing, Tombola carried on. "And this little fellow is my best friend," she said. "Since that oversized chimp got himself married that is."

She unravelled a parrot, named Squawky, from a pile of jungle leaves. She shook him, but the parrot didn't move so she chucked him inside the tent.

"He'll be all right tomorrow," she said. "He's got jet lag I expect. It was a terrible flight you know. I had a heck of a job keeping all this lot on me broomstick."

"You came all the way from Africa on a broomstick!" gasped Simon.

"Well of course I did, ducky. I couldn't afford to

pay fares for *this* menagerie!"

Simon suddenly realized what the black "cloud" had been, and the flapping noises they'd heard outside Valdini's. He must tell his mother. On second thoughts, she might not believe him.

Meanwhile, Angelica had just arrived at Simon's house. She was stunned with disappointment when she found he was out. Simon's mother explained that he had gone to visit an old lady who lived at the other end of the town.

"Oh how kind of him!" cried Angelica. "I love looking after old ladies too. My mummy says old people are terribly important."

Simon's mother interrupted her hastily, and suggested she should go and visit this particular old lady, where she would find Simon.

"My mummy might not like me walking down strange roads," piped Angelica. "But if I get lost, Simon can come and find me, and that would be super!"

And off she skipped. "How pleased Simon will be to see me," she said to herself. "I'll be able to help him. It's a beautiful thing to help the old. But of course it's jolly hard as well. Some old people are fussy. And bossy. And some of them are *hideously* ugly. Or fat and boring. Or skinny and cross. Or *ghastly*. It's a good job I'm kind. And I can boss them back too."

Still talking to herself, she turned the corner and gasped, "What a horrid little street! And, good gracious, this old lady must like playing cowboys and Indians, there's a tatty-looking tent in the garden!"

She skipped up to the garden gate and looked over. At that moment, Tombola and the witch emerged from the tent to collect the snakes from the box, and George shot up the drainpipe and disappeared over the roof.

Angelica froze on the spot. She could not believe what she was seeing, — two hideous witches, a black panther jumping over the house, and a box of dangerous man-eating snakes! And there were Simon and Jimmy, just standing there. Mesmerized with fear no doubt. She opened her small pink mouth and gave out an ear-splitting scream.

The scream roused Squawky, who imagined he was still flying over stormy waters. "Turn left at the Bay of Biscay!" he shrieked.

Simon grinned at the witch as he watched the fleeing figure of Angelica, and said, "It's been quite a good day really."

"Is that Sugar Plum, Angelica?" asked the witch, cackling maliciously.

The Stolen Wand

Simon's mother was just finishing speaking on the phone when Simon and Jimmy arrived home. Angelica's mother had had to call in the doctor. It seemed that Angelica had a fever and was talking nonsense.

Simon shuffled and went slightly red.

"Apparently," said his mother, "Angelica had seen two witches, a black panther, and a whole garden full of dangerous snakes."

"Oh, she means the witch and her sister. It was only George who jumped over the roof, and the snakes were just pets," explained Simon.

"Really, Simon!" said his mother. "You and your imagination! Anyway, whatever's the matter with Angelica, I hope you don't catch it."

Simon and Jimmy escaped upstairs to play with Simon's soldiers.

"I suppose I could get used to Tombola," said

Jimmy, attacking one of Simon's soldiers, "but it's the *snakes*!"

"Squawky sounds nice, though," said Simon, attacking one of Jimmy's men.

"It probably pecks," added Jimmy, gloomily.

"One good thing, though," said Simon. "It got Angelica out of the way."

"She'll probably die," said Jimmy.

Simon looked a bit uncomfortable at this. Then he decided that Angelica was far too bossy to die. And they went on with their game.

The peace was broken by the sound of a rumpus downstairs, and the witch came bursting in through the bedroom door, looking slightly frantic.

"Guess what!" she puffed.

"George has eaten all Tombola's snakes," said Simon.

"Worse than that," gasped the witch, "I wish he had done. They're getting on my nerves. No, actually, one of the snakes did get up the electric cleaner and I had to put it into reverse to blow him out, and all *these* shot out as well!"

"All what?" asked Jimmy, grinning nervously.

Furtively, the witch rummaged in her handbag and produced a large pile of electricity bills.

"They must've got sucked up when we got Foxy's adverts out of the letterboxes."

"Wow!" gasped Simon. "My mother's been wondering when hers was coming."

"We'll get *killed* when they find out," moaned Jimmy.

"I'm too young to die!" mocked the witch.

"We'll just have to deliver them all again, I suppose," Simon sighed.

"I'm sick of being a bloomin' postman," the witch grumbled. "And anyway, I'm not going near that mad woman's house again. If she sees me coming, she'll probably say I didn't clean her stupid cat properly. Or she'll say I stole the fleas off it."

"Well we can't just keep electricity bills. They're important," said Simon.

"We could just put the whole lot back in the Post Office letterbox. Then the real postman will have to do them," said Jimmy.

Simon and the witch stared at Jimmy open-mouthed.

"Isn't that strange! I was just going to say that myself," lied the witch. She squashed the bills back into her handbag, except for the one which was addressed to Lady Fox-Custard. She gave the boys a sly grin.

"I've got an idea about this one," she tittered. And she left, looking a lot more cheerful.

"She's up to something," Jimmy shivered.

Meanwhile, Lady Fox-Custard had a plan of her own. She had decided to start a holiday club.

"It will be for *nice* little children," she told Hopkins. "No rough, wild boys. There's a sweet little child called Angelica who has just arrived in the town. She would make a suitable friend for Cuthbert. Her father is terribly high up."

Cuthbert, who had been deep inside a comic, looked up in alarm.

"And then, there's Sally, of course," his aunt continued, "and I daresay I'll be able to think of a few h'other educated sorts of children."

She started to fuss around, importantly.

"Hopkins," she scolded. "Don't just stand there like a pot statue. Put some things out."

"Things, Ma'am?"

"Little games, and paper and pencils for me club. Don't leave me to do *everything*," complained Lady Fox-Custard.

"Whatever you say, Ma'mm," sighed Hopkins, going off to look in the attic.

Lady Fox-Custard made a few phone calls. She rang Angelica's mother.

"I'm starting a little holiday club," she said in her best voice. "I thought your *dear* little daughter would like to join. I'll send the Rolls for her . . . Oh, yes of course. I *h'always* use brown bread for me sandwiches . . ."

"Oh gosh!" thought Cuthbert to himself. "This is the worst idea she's ever had. And she hasn't invited any of my friends."

The following afternoon, a few "suitable" children began to arrive, and wearily, Cuthbert went to meet them at the door. When Angelica turned up, she immediately fell in love with Cuthbert.

"How sweet of you to let me join your holiday club," she cooed.

"I didn't." Cuthbert was horrified. "It was my aunt's idea."

"Yes, but you still let me," beamed Angelica. "I bet you're a lord or something, aren't you? I bet you've even met the Queen, haven't you?"

Cuthbert said he'd just go and hang up Angelica's

cardigan for her.

They all settled down at their tables. It was very dull, especially as Lady Fox-Custard kept saying "Shush." She didn't want to have to turn off the television.

"What a good idea to have a club," said Sally, filling in a boring crossword puzzle. "It's much better than just playing around in this hot weather."

Cuthbert looked longingly out at the sunshine.

"I love it too," giggled Angelica, who was colouring in a clown. She shuffled her chair nearer to Cuthbert's, smiling at him widely, and whispered, "Please may I have a little tiny lend of your yellow?"

"Shush!" said Lady Fox-Custard, who was trying to listen to the television.

The other children were afraid even to blow their noses. It was just like being back in school.

And so a perfectly good, sunny afternoon dragged on, completely wasted as far as Cuthbert was concerned.

Back at the witch's house, Tombola and the witch were swopping magic spells and boasting to each other.

"Your spell book's tatty and old fashioned," Tombola said. She pulled a damp wad of spells out of her pocket, blew a few patches of elephant dust off them and said, "Here, try an African one."

"I don't want no more noisy parrots appearing,"

said the witch, cautiously. She waved her wand, and instantly, George turned into a giant rubber plant.

"See!" exclaimed Tombola. "My spells are dead modern. Now all you need to do is water him."

The witch was highly indignant.

"You fat clown!" she bellowed. "How can I fly round on me broomstick with a stupid rubber plant sitting behind me instead of a cat! What if I bumped into Hatty the Howl, or Minnie the Moan? They'd drop clean out of the sky, laughing at me. Turn George back again at once!"

"Boring," sulked Tombola, doing as she was told. "I thought you'd be glad not to have that flea-ridden monstrocity following you around."

The two witches felt a little bored. George bit a small hole out of Tombola's shoe and skulked off. Then the witch remembered she still had Lady Fox-Custard's electricity bill in her pocket. She began to grin.

"I've thought of something really funny we can do. We'll dress up as electricity men and go and cut off old Foxy's electricity. She'll go bananas!"

She magicked up two important-looking uniforms and they set off at a run towards Horty Hall, cackling with enormous amusement all the way.

"Mind the begonias!" she warned Tombola, stepping on one and ringing the bell at the same time.

Hopkins opened the door. "Yes?" he said.

Good! thought the witch. He doesn't recognize us. He thinks we're a couple of fellas.

"We're from the Electricity Board," she told him. "We've come to cut her Ladyship off."

"Cut her off," repeated Tombola, who was holding a large pair of garden shears she had just helped herself to.

Hopkins led them into the drawing room where the children were.

"These two gentlemen have come to cut you off," he announced to Lady Fox-Custard.

Lady Fox-Custard had a chocolate halfway into her mouth and her mouth stayed open.

"To cut what orf?" she managed to say.

"Your electricity, Ma'am," said the witch. "You haven't paid your bill."

"I didn't *GET* me bill!" shrieked Lady Fox-Custard, forgetting that she was in the middle of running a holiday club.

The children had stopped playing and were waiting with interest to see what would happen next.

"Ah!" said the witch, "they all say that — don't they, 'Arry?"

"Yes, they all say that," echoed Tombola. "They say, 'Please please, I'm only an old lady!'"

"I would *never* say that!" snooted Lady Fox-Custard, "but I do 'appen to have a huge fresh salmon in the freezer, sent to me specially from Scotland by Lord Mackintosh Macrae. It'll go orf."

"And they all say that as well," scoffed the witch, enjoying herself hugely.

"Yes," sniggered Tombola. "They all say they've got huge salmons from Lord Mackintosh Macrae."

"Will you please stop talking like a parrot!" the witch spat at her sister.

Then she noticed the garden shears Tombola was stil carrying. "You can't cut off her electricity with *those*, you ninny. You'll get yourself electromuckuted."

"What funny men," giggled Angelica. She was enjoying the holiday club.

The two witches stomped out into the corridor in

search of the electricity meter. Then they waved their magic wands at it and the freezer and the television went off and the witches disappeared.

Lady Fox-Custard screamed and Hopkins told the children he thought it was time for them to be going. Lady Fox-Custard's chins were all wobbling together.

Angelica looked disappointed. "Thank you for having me," she piped. She glanced dreamily at Cuthbert. "I'll definitely be coming again. Lots and lots of times. And she went to fetch her cardigan.

"I think there was something very odd about those electricity men," Sally whispered in Lady Fox-Custard's ear. "I think the fat one could have been the witch."

Lady Fox-Custard's eyes went into two little slits, and lots of suspicious and nasty thoughts rattled round in her head. Angelica was quite frightened and said she couldn't wait for the car, she must go at once. It was such a shame when she had been getting on so well with Cuthbert. He had much nicer manners than Simon, she thought.

Tombola and the witch were back in the witch's kitchen and were rolling round the floor like two black puddings, laughing.

"I see what you mean about that potty woman," said Tombola, hooting. "Her face when the television went phoot! It was like a custard pie after someone had sat on it."

The witch was proud of her brilliant idea, and started boasting about lots of other terrible things she had done, until Tombola began to get sick of her.

Next day, Lady Fox-Custard went down to the garden shed and rummaged out the gardener's old mackintosh. She also found a floppy hat which she pulled on. She had been awake all night, fuming and seething, and she had come up with a master plan. The more she had thought about it, the more she was sure that the fat electricity man had really been the witch in disguise. She determined to steal the witch's wand. Of course, it was probably just a dirty old stick, but whatever it was, she knew the witch would be annoyed to lose it.

She stood on the corner of the witch's street and watched the witch's front door for several hours. She was glad *she* didn't live in such a mean street. Even the cats and dogs looked mean. At long last, the witch and Tombola came out. They were pulling a shopping trolley so Lady Fox-Custard guessed they'd be gone for some time. As soon as they were out of sight, Lady Fox-Custard scurried inside the witch's house. She was horrified at the gloom and clutter. It would take her hours to find the wand and she didn't have much time. She started by treading on George who yowled furiously and dug his claws into her leg. Lady Fox-Custard put up with the pain, rather than make a

noise. But Squawky didn't mind at all making a noise
and screeched, "Custard tart! Custard tart!"

"Oh my goodness!" wailed Lady Fox-Custard.
"What a terrible place this is! I must hurry up and get
out."

And she hurried straight into a pan of soup which
slopped all over the carpet. She tried to scoop it up
with a spoon, but it was taking her too long, so she
topped up the soup with tap water. Looking for the
wand was like looking for a needle in a haystack.
Perhaps the dratted woman had taken it with her. All
the while, George glared nastily at her and growled,
unpleasantly. He watched her pulling open drawers
and nosing into cupboards. Suddenly, Lady Fox-

61

Custard spotted the wand on the top of the mantel-piece. It had been staring at her all the time. Delighted, she snatched it up and ran out of the door. Unfortunately, Tombola's snakes, who had been shut up all morning, slithered after her and escaped in all directions through the cabbage patch.

At that moment, the two witches returned from the shops. The witch was just in time to see the back of Lady Fox-Custard as she sped round the corner. Obviously, a tramp had been in her front garden. Then she found her front door was still half open and hurried inside to see what was missing.

"You've got nothing worth pinching," chortled Tombola.

The witch had to agree she hadn't. She picked up the pan of soup from the floor, heated it up and served out the lunch.

"Tastes like tap water!" spat the witch.

"I bet you have *much* better soup in Africa," the witch hinted. The witch was beginning to get thoroughly fed up with her sister. Tombola was rude about George, yet she couldn't keep her own pets in order. As well as that she boasted too much.

"Arrrrrrgh!" screamed Tombola.

"Well if you don't like it, don't finish it," sulked the witch.

"Not the soup—me snakes!" Tombola wailed. "I left them here under this cushion."

"That tramp's stolen them! What d'you bet?" said the witch, half pleased and half annoyed. I *knew* he looked shifty. He must've been a snake pincher."

"Let's get after him!" shrieked Tombola.

And the two witches dashed out of the house.

When Lady Fox-Custard arrived back at Horty Hall she was irritated to see that the children had turned up for another afternoon of messing about with bits of paper and silly games. What had possessed her to start a stupid holiday club? She hung up her old mackintosh and hat, gave the children a sickly grin and sat down, exhausted, only to be set upon by Cuthbert, reminding her that it was his birthday in a few days.

"I'll buy you another puzzle book," she said, faintly. She was still shaking with horror at the dangerous expedition she had just been on. But Cuthbert wanted a party. He had never had a party in the whole of his life. He wanted to invite all his friends. The Duke and Duchess of Do-Nuthin had sent him enough money to pay for it. Lady Fox-Custard was afraid of Cuthbert's parents disapproving of her, so she had to agree.

"I think parties are a silly waste of money," she said, "but I suppose if you *must* have one then I suppose you must. She ground her teeth and pulled a face like a squashed banana, adding, "and get those noisy children out of me house."

Cuthbert wrote out the invitations at once, and Hopkins was sent off to deliver them.

When Simon received his, he was delighted. Even Jimmy had been invited. They dashed round to the witch's to see if she had an invitation too, but the witch was out, so the boys went to look for her and found her with Tombola in Valdini's. The witch was just showing off to her sister what an important customer she was. When she heard about the birthday party she was furious.

"I didn't get no invitation," she bellowed. "I'm just as good as anyone else. That fat Fox with ten chins and the baggy tummy is jealous of me, that's what it is! She thinks if I go to the rotten party, everyone will be admiring *me* instead of her!"

"You're no oil painting either!" tittered Tombola, and went off to look at the food. She could not decide which ice cream to choose. Perhaps she would try them all.

"The spaghetti's very nice," Valdini was saying.

"The whaty? asked Tombola.

"Spaghetti," said Valdini, proudly stirring his prize recipe.

Tombola peered into the pan, curiously. Then her purple face turned a frightening green. "My darling snakes!" she screamed. "They've been stolen, and boiled in tomato juice until they are dead. And as well as that, they've *shrunk!*"

"Ma'am, please," pleaded Valdini, terrified and very upset.

"Snake thief!" yelled Tombola, pouring the spaghetti into her hat and storming out.

"She's mad," was all the witch said. "I'm sick of her tantrums."

When the witch arrived home with the boys, Tombola had gone. Tent and all.

"Thank goodness for that," said the witch. "Peace at last."

The Witch's Holiday Club

Simon and Jimmy talked excitedly about Cuthbert's party. It was not often they got inside Horty Hall, with all its large rooms and nooks and crannies. Sally of course, as she kept pointing out, was well used to the hall.

"I suppose it's because I have nice manners," she said.

Hopkins had invited Valdini to do the catering, and he was strutting round telling everbody that he was "bigly proud". Only the witch was unexcited.

"I think it's a dump," she said. "The chairs fall to bits when you sit on 'em; her furniture's dead old and antwacky. I've seen posher looking bus depots."

Simon giggled. He thought the witch was very funny when she was jealous. He was much more interested in where Tombola had gone.

"Back to Africa, I hope," said the witch. And forgot about her. "I'll make us both a nice fizzy drink," she said, reaching for her wand. She went white with shock when she discovered that it had vanished. "I've been robbed!" she screamed, frantically.

George miaowed and tried to pull a face which looked like Lady Fox-Custard's, but the witch slapped him for making fun.

"Perhaps Tombola took it," said Simon.

"Never," said the witch. "She's a trouble maker and a big nuisance. And her clothes are a sight, and her pets have no manners, but that's one thing she wouldn't do. No witch would ever steal a wand from another witch. It must've been that tramp we saw."

Simon didn't know what to say, except that he had better be going: his mother wanted to take him to town for a new shirt.

The day of the party dawned and the excited children arrived at the hall. Hopkins stood at the door, announcing them as they came. "Master James," he said.

Jimmy looked all round him, puzzled.

"He means *you*," laughed Cuthbert.

Then Angelica appeared. Her hair had been done up in corkscrew ringlets and her dress was like a pink cloud. Sally who was just wearing an ordinary skirt and blouse, eyed her up and down, enviously. Angelica would never be able to play properly with all those frills. But Angelica seemed to have huge fun.

Every time she crashed down in musical chairs, her frills flounced around her prettily. Even Cuthbert looked a little impressed.

"What about playing hide and seek in the garden," Sally suggested. A little mud on those ridiculous frills would bring Angelica down a peg or two.

The boys readily agreed, and before Lady Fox-Custard could protest, they had charged off in all directions. Simon and Cuthbert made a bee line for the garden where the most bushes grew.

"Pssst!" said a voice from nowhere.

Simon was shocked. He knew the witch was hiding somewhere close by; gatecrashing the party.

"Over here," chortled the witch.

The witch was lying flat in a bed of daisies.

"Let's go and hide in the ditch," she giggled.

She set off at breakneck speed across the garden, and dived joyfully into a very muddy ditch. Mud flew everywhere.

"My new shirt!" gasped Simon.

"Mine's gone a funny colour too," giggled Cuthbert. "My party was getting awfully boring." He laughed so much, that Jimmy who was 'it' soon found them. They all marched back to the house to start a new game.

When Lady Fox-Custard saw the state her little nephew had got himself into, she was livid. "I'm stopping this rough game," she said. "Sit down at

once and we'll get on with the tea."

She rang the bell for Hopkins.

The tea was not as she expected. Instead of cucumber sandwiches and little jellies, Hopkins wheeled in a huge assortment of pizzas, spaghetti on toast, meat balls with garlic, and other "rubbish."

"How common!" she shuddered. "Who on earth did you employ to do the catering?" Fortunately, she had bought the cake herself, and although a little on the small side, it at least looked normal. Stretching her mouth into a tight smile she began to sing.

"Happy birthday to you . . ."

"Happy birthday to you," sang the witch in a

cracked voice. Her nose was just visible, poking through the window.

"Hurray! It's the witch!" cried Cuthbert.

"Can I come in, Your Snooty-Ship?" the witch asked.

"You certainly can *not*!" bellowed Lady Fox-Custard, all her chins wobbling at once.

A small plaintive voice came from the door. "Nobody's come to look for me," said Angelica. "I've been hiding in a super corner in the cloakroom, and look what I've found in a dirty old pocket."

She came tripping in like a fairy, waving the witch's magic wand.

"That's *mine*!" shrieked the witch. "Now I know who that tramp was snooping round my abode."

And her nose flashed green and red.

Angelica flew. And Lady Fox-Custard went beetroot and decided she'd better faint at once, but not before she had screamed, "The Holiday Club is CLOSED!"

Next day, the boys collected in the witch's house. They were all talking about the party. Lady Fox-Custard had discovered that it was Valdini who had done the catering, and she was on the warpath, even more determined to have his café closed down.

"And the holiday club's closed," moaned Jimmy.

"But you weren't even in it," Simon pointed out.

"He should be jolly glad," said Cuthbert. "It was dead boring."

The witch was picking at a spider salad and listening to the boys. "What a lot of moaning minnies you are," she scolded. "That toffee-nosed custard isn't the only one who can start a holiday club."

"Who else could?" asked Jimmy.

"*I* could, of course," said the witch. "I can start anything I like. I've just started one now and you're all in it."

She rummaged in her drawer for some scissors and cut out little cardboard badges on which she wrote, WITCH'S HOLIDAY CLUB, and pinned one on each boy. She made another one for herself which said KAPTUN.

71

"Now what?" asked Jimmy.

The witch looked irritated. She hadn't thought about what they could actually do.

"Not silly games I hope," said Cuthbert. "I've had enought of those."

"Certainly not," said the witch. "We'll climb some mountains. Everest perhaps. And we'll go fishing for whales, and visit the zoo, and . . ."

"What about camping," interrupted Simon.

"What's that?" asked the witch, a bit miffed at having her large ideas interrupted.

"It's living in a tent, and having camp fires, and cooking in the open," Simon explained. He had a tent at home; all they needed was somewhere to put it. Everyone trudged back to Simon's house to have a look at his tent. To Simon's annoyance, Angelica was there to greet him. When she saw the witch, she was about to give one of her special screams again, but she noticed to her astonishment that Simon's mother not only just stood there, but even said "Hullo," and the witch said, "Hullo, Mrs Woman," back.

The witch looked Angelica up and down, from the frill on her dress to the top of her lemon bow.

"So *this* is the sugar plum," she said.

Angelica got braver and moved a little closer. She didn't want Simon and Cuthbert to think she was a baby. Also, she wanted to know why they were all wearing badges. So Simon explained about the witch's club.

"I want to join too," begged Angelica.

"I'm sure you can," said Simon's mother, before anyone had time to say she couldn't.

Then Simon got out his tent.

"It's titchy," said Jimmy.

"What's it for" said Cuthbert. "A flea?"

"Well at least it's something for us to play in," sulked Simon.

"Perhaps if I ask her nicely, Lady Fox-Custard would let you camp in the garden at Horty Hall," said his mother. "I'll ring her up now."

"Camping? In my garden!" choked Lady Fox-Custard over the phone." But I'm finished with holiday clubs – and boys."

Simon's mother said that the children could stay well away from the house, and they'd be in the fresh air. More than that, it would keep them away from undesirable cafés.

Lady Fox-Custard thought about that. A cunning look crept over her face. "Keep them away from cafés, you say?" she said. "Very well then, but I want no fires, no tree felling, and no fishing in me pond."

"Of course not," agreed Simon's mother.

Excitedly, the children trooped along to Horty Hall garden and put up their tent. It was really cosy. When they had finished playing squashed sardines in it, they sat around in the sunshine and the witch told them long exciting stories about herself. Most of the stories were untrue, but nobody minded.

Now and again, Lady Fox-Custard spied on them with binoculars, then she grew bored and ordered Hopkins to bring her some tea. Obviously, nothing terrible was going to happen. The children arranged to meet again and they all went home.

"Did you think that was good?" the witch asked Simon.

"Yes, I thought it was great," said Simon.

"I thought it was a bit boring," said the witch.

All this time, Tombola had been looking for a new site where she could pitch her tent. She had found her snakes amongst the cabbages, ticked them off for being naughty, and fastened them safely onto her broomstick. She had been flying around for days, peering down for a suitable place to land. Suddenly, she spotted a large green space. There were trees, and rose bushes, and a dinky little pond. Not only that, there was a small tent. Obviously it was all right to camp there. She zoomed down and landed with a crash.

"This is just the very place!" she exclaimed.

Squawky found an owl he thought he could be friendly with and the snakes went for an evening slither. Tombola felled a tree, lit a fire, and collected some water from the pond, choosing the best of the goldfish for her supper. She looked around her new

home with pleasure. The witch could keep her rotten little garden. This one was fit for a lady.

Next morning, the witch and the children were keen to get back to their camp. Simon's mother had made a huge pile of sandwiches for him to share. The sun was hotter than ever, and it was going to be a wonderful day. Cuthbert was waiting for them at the gates of Horty Hall, but he was looking panic stricken.

"Ssh!" he whispered." There's something big and strange at the bottom of the garden. It looks like a grey monster of some sort."

Angelica screamed.

"He said, 'Ssh'!" scolded the witch. "Come on,

campers. Let's stalk it."

They crawled across the grass, silently, except for the witch, who was heavy and kept kneeling on twigs which cracked with a noise like gunfire. Then a familiar voice rang out. Tombola was singing,

"I'm a jolly camper,
Sitting in the sun,
Frying slugs and sausages
Is lots of super fun."

"At ease, scouts," said the witch. "It's just that crackpot sister of mine. What a bloomin' cheek she's got!"

"You're only jealous," mocked Tombola, slurping a spoonful of sizzling slugs, "just 'cos I've found somewhere posh to live."

"But this is my aunt's garden," Cuthbert told her.

"Oh heck," Tombola said. "Oh well, I'm not doing any harm, am I?"

Cuthbert looked at the pine tree which had been chopped down, the large camp fire, and the half empty goldfish pond. Perhaps if he didn't mention it, his aunt might not notice.

"Oh please, please, let's stay," begged Angelica. "I'm getting really brave with witches. Look," she took a tiny step towards Tombola who stared at her as if she was some strange bird of paradise.

"All right," agreed Cuthbert. "But Tombola had better keep out of sight, and we'll have to play something quiet."

"Like rugby," suggested the witch.

"*Not* like rugby," said Simon. "We could have a treasure hunt with clues."

So the witch made up some very hard clues.

To the boys' surprise, Angelica turned out to be quite good at working out clues.

LOOK FOR GOLD UNDERWATER

she read. "That's easy. It means the goldfish in the pond."

The children gathered around the pond to look for the next clue.

At this point, Lady Fox-Custard looked out of the window. "Thank goodness for that," she said to Hopkins. "Cuthbert is teaching those poor deprived children about nature and pond life."

Tombola, on the other hand, was not so pleased. She would rather have had the garden to herself. The children were everywhere, buzzing this way and that like bees. Her snakes, who were supposed to be on holiday, were in danger of being trodden on. Crossly, she pulled up a dozen or so raspberry canes and tossed them on the fire. A cloud of black smoke billowed up into the sky.

Lady Fox-Custard wiffled her nose like a rabbit and scowled. "Hopkins," she bawled. "Can you smell smoke?"

"I'm sure it's just the gardener, burning rubbish," mumbled Hopkins, who had now found out what was going on.

Angelica had just worked out another clue. It said,

IN BETWEEN TWO HARD PILLOWS

"I bet that means PILLARS," she trilled, pleased at the astonished looks the boys were giving her. They were thinking, she was sure, that she was terribly clever, as well as being awfully pretty. She skipped gaily across the lawn towards the front door and looked round the base of the pillars.

One of Tombola's snakes had been enjoying a sunny snooze against the warm stone and huffily slithered off inside the house and made for the warmth of the sofa. He curled up next to a fat lady who looked, he thought, like a magnificent cushion. Lady Fox-Custard reached out her hand to get another chocolate and picked up the snake instead.

"Arrrrrrrgh!" she screamed in terror. "A *snake!*"

"Where?" yelled Tombola, bursting through the window.

Tombola grabbed the snake and charged down the garden with it. It seemed her darling little pets weren't safe anywhere. Lady Fox-Custard didn't feel safe either. She tottered to the phone.

"Nine-nine-nine!" she spluttered.

"What's up?" sighed Constable Scuff, who had

just taken one bite of his cheese sandwich.

"I'm being attacked by an enormous, poisonous snake!" yelled Lady Fox-Custard.

Constable Scuff scratched his head and thought for a minute. Then he got out his notebook and found a new pen. "For one moment, I thought you said a poisonous snake!" he laughed. "You've eaten a poisonous *cake*, have you, well . . ."

"I *did* say a snake, you dozy bluebottle!" screamed Lady Fox-Custard. "And there's a mad witch in my garden too."

Wearily, Constable Scuff climbed into his police car, taking his cheese sandwich with him.

The children escaped back into the garden. "I don't suppose we'll be able to play here any more," said Simon gloomily to the others.

"And it's all my sister's fault," spat the witch.

Tombola was counting her snakes and packing them into a box. She pulled Squawky down out of a tree and packed him, also. Just then, she heard a police siren in the distance. With one tug, she collapsed her tent and parcelled all her belongings onto her broomstick. She zoomed up over the trees and headed back for Africa. The jungle was a lot more peaceful, she decided.

Constable Scuff arrived and headed down the garden. There was no Tombola, no tent, no parrot, and no snakes, – only the remains of a tree and some

ash where a bonfire had been, probably where the gardener had been burning rubbish.

The witch grinned, slyly. She jerked her head towards Horty Hall.

"Her Barmy-Ship keeps seeing things," she tittered. "Today it was snakes. Yesterday it was elephants. The day before that it was blue-nosed baboons. It's sad really."

"It's a waste of police time. That's what it is!" growled Constable Scuff. And he shot off back to the police station.

A Storm in a Teacup

All this trouble, Lady Fox-Custard decided, was due to the witch. If the witch hadn't come to live in the town, the children would have been having a nice, ordinary sort of holiday: sitting quietly with their books, going for little walks, and perhaps playing safely in the park. But because of the witch they were up to all sorts of rough pranks. Not one of them had shown any surprise when Tombola's snake had slithered into her house, or her garden had been ruined by that mad woman. And to top it all, they were still being led, almost daily into that dirty, common, and beetle infested café, Valdini's. It was her *duty* to do something about it all. She decided to get Sally to help her.

Sally was surprised to be invited to Horty Hall again so soon. She was even more surprised at being invited to sit down for tea.

"I want you to do a very important job for me,"

said Lady Fox-Custard. "I know you won't like it, but I want you to follow the children into Valdini's café, and then you must ask to join the witch's holiday club. After that, you must tell me everything that dreadful old woman is up to, and everything that goes on in that disgusting café."

"D'you mean SPY!?" gasped Sally.

Lady Fox-Custard winced. "I don't like to use that word," she said. "But yes, that's exactly what I mean."

Sally was secretly delighted and agreed to be a spy.

The next morning, the witch and the children went to Valdini's for refreshments.

Cuthbert was surprised that his aunt had suddenly allowed him to go.

"Perhaps she's getting nicer," he said.

"And perhaps she isn't," grunted the witch.

She didn't trust Lady Fox-Custard as far as she could throw her, and Lady Fox-Custard was such a fat wobbly lady, the witch didn't think she could have thrown her one inch.

"You said we could go to the zoo," reminded Simon.

"Haven't got no money," said the witch.

Neither did anyone else.

Jimmy began to grumble. He didn't even have enough for another lemonade.

At that moment, Sally arrived. She smiled sweetly

at everybody and sat down. "I've been so bored," she said, "I would just love to join your club, if I may."

"You mayn't," muttered the witch.

But Angelica was delighted to see Sally. "Oh please, please, lovely kind witch," she begged. "Let Sally join. It's terrible being the only girl."

"But she's a trouble maker," said Simon. "She tried to get Mr Valdini into trouble."

"I'm sorry about that," lied Sally. "I made a mistake. I think this café looks lovely. That ice cream looks marvellous, and the spaghetti smells wonderful." She smiled broadly at Valdini, who smiled back, nervously.

Angelica pleaded so hard, the witch grew irritated and gave in.

Now that she had wormed her way into the holiday club, Sally wanted to know what they were doing. Angelica told her they had no pocket money, so they weren't doing anything.

"We'll have to think of ways of MAKING money," the witch said.

"Making money," thought Sally. "That's against the law for a start!"

"I could rob a bank I suppose," cackled the witch, rolling round on her chair with amusement.

Sally was listening carefully to every word the witch said, so that she could report back to Lady Fox-Custard.

"People get lots of money when they go round with collecting boxes," said Jimmy.

"But they wouldn't give money to little kids," the witch said. "They wouldn't know if they were real money boxes or just pretend ones."

"Or we could just all ask for more pocket money," suggested Cuthbert, simply.

"Oh yes!" scoffed the witch. "I could ask my mummy!"

The thought of the witch having a mummy made all the children fall about laughing.

Then Simon suggested they could do useful jobs for people, like they did in the boy scouts.

"I'm sure my mother would be jolly glad to pay to have our house cleaned.

"That's not a bad idea," said the witch. "I could make some green overalls, and we could call ourselves the Holiday Handy Helpers."

Everyone agreed that Simon's idea would work. They would call at the witch's house in the afternoon to get their uniforms and whatever else they needed.

When Simon got home, he told his mother that they were going to clean the house.

"That's if you don't mind," he said. "And it won't cost you much."

"I like that!" laughed his mother. "You should tidy up for nothing. Still, I suppose your bedroom could do with a going over. I should think it will take the Holiday Handy Helpers a week just to pick up your socks!"

Sally in the meantime, was ringing Lady Fox-Custard.

"I've found out a couple of interesting things," she was saying. "The witch is definitely up to something crooked. She talked about *making* money, and the next minute she said she was going to rob a bank!"

"I *knew* it!" exclaimed Lady Fox-Custard, pursing her mouth up into a nasty little button.

She jumped into her Rolls Royce and drove down to the police station. She hit the bell on the counter and Constable Scuff appeared.

Lady Fox-Custard pulled her hat down low over her eyes, peering round to see if she was being overheard.

"I've got something shocking to tell you," she hissed.

Constable Scuff groaned to himself. He was sick and tired of Lady Fox-Custard.

"I have reason to believe that someone is going to rob the bank," said Lady Fox-Custard.

Constable Scuff cheered up at this.

"*Who*?" he cried.

"It's that old witch woman at the other end of town," Lady Fox-Custard told him.

"Oh her," sighed Constable Scuff, very disappointed. "That old lady couldn't rob a piggy bank."

"Listen, you," screeched Lady Fox-Custard, grabbing the policeman by his collar. "It's not up to you to say who could and who couldn't rob a bank, it's up to you to see they jolly well *don't*"

"Yes Ma'am," croaked Constable Scuff, terrified.

"Well get on with your job then," snapped Lady Fox-Custard, and stamped off.

Meanwhile, the children had arrived at Simon's house, ready to clean out his room. They were dressed in green overalls with *Holiday Handy Helpers* embroidered on them. The witch was rattling with buckets and brushes and had dusters hung around her like flags. Simon's mother looked a little alarmed, but let them in.

"You girls get started," said the witch, "the boys and I will just have a quick game of Monopoly."

Sally was about to exclaim, "What a cheek!" Then she remembered she was supposed to be spying, so she said nothing.

The Monopoly game went on for several hours. So long in fact, that Sally and Angelica had finished the whole room.

"Oh gosh!" said the witch. "We meant to help. Didn't we, boys?"

She had won the Monopoly game, anyway, and her pockets were bulging with houses and hotels, so she decided she might as well go. She left so swiftly, Sally had difficulty keeping up with her. But she was just in time to spot the witch coming out of the bank. The

witch's handbag was bulging and there was a five pound note sticking out of the top of it.

"There must be *thousands* in that bag!" thought Sally, still trailing the witch at a distance.

Just round the corner of the witch's house, lurked Constable Scuff. He was rocking on his heels and pretending to look at the sky.

"I think that witch woman has just robbed the bank," Sally told him.

"Hey up!" said Constable Scuff.

And he and Sally peered cautiously through the witch's window.

"Well, George," the witch was saying, "we'll have some lovely chips for our supper tonight."

She opened her handbag, took out the five pound note which she'd just got at the bank, and a large bag of potatoes.

Sally went very red and Constable Scuff sighed heavily and went off to phone Lady Fox-Custard.

"You silly man!" scoffed Lady Fox-Custard. "The money was probably hidden inside the potatoes. Keep following her."

Constable Scuff followed the witch all week and she did nothing wicked at all. Most of the time, she went into the café with the children. Constable Scuff thought if he had to eat any more spaghetti, he would burst.

The holiday club was talking about new ways the

Holiday Handy Helpers could help people.

"We could have a bingo party in the café," said Simon. "That would bring lots of new customers into Valdini's and we'd get a bit more pocket money as well."

"And Valdini could make millions of ice creams!" cried the witch. "I'll make him a rich man!" she shouted.

Constable Scuff pricked up his ears at this. He took out his notebook and wrote, THE WITCH WOMAN IS GOING TO MAKE VALDINI A RICH MAN. And he shot off to phone Lady Fox-Custard.

"Right!" said Lady Fox-Custard, "I'm going to get that café closed down, once and for all. It's a den for crooks. I'll have a word with the mayor and we'll catch that woman red-handed when she hands the money over to Valdini."

She rang the mayor and ordered him to come to tea the next day. "I have something very serious to tell you," she said.

"Oh," said the mayor, polishing his gold chain and hoping there would be plenty of cream cakes for tea.

All this time, Cuthbert, who had been sitting in a corner, reading *Harder Problems Are Fun Too*, heard what his aunt was planning, and ran off to warn the witch.

"Hopkins is going to serve the tea on the lawn," Cuthbert said, "so we'll be able to hide in the bushes and hear what Aunty is going to tell the mayor."

"I've got a better idea," chuckled the witch. "Your aunty won't have time to tell the mayor *anything*."

She didn't tell Cuthbert what her idea was, but next day, she put on her best coat – the one which had buttons shaped like cat's claws, and flew over London to the BBC.

When she arrived, she raced straight past the girl on the desk towards the lift.

"Excuse me," said the girl on the desk.

"Why?" asked the witch. "What have you done?"

"You can't just go up there," the girl told her.

"Got to," puffed the witch. "I'm doin' the weather forecast. Didn't no one tell you?"

And she disappeared into the lift.

The weather man, who was called Mr Fish, was just about to read the weather forecast on television, when the witch burst into the studio.

"Sorry I'm late, Mr Sardine," she panted.

She waddled across to the chart on the wall and said, "Is this it then?"

"This can't be right," stuttered Mr Fish. "No one told me anyone new was coming."

"Didn't they?" said the witch. "Fancy no one telling you."

She studied the weather chart with her eyeglass.

"Now what are you doing?" asked Mr Fish.

"I'm looking for someone," the witch told him.

Mr Fish laughed.

"My dear woman," he said. "You can't see *people* on that map!"

"Can't you?" said the witch, amazed. "I can." She peered closer. "There's the Queen . . . Oops! One of the corgis has just run off! And there's the Prime Minister. Ah! – now I can see old Lady Fox-Custard."

"Where?" gasped Mr Fish, astonished.

"Underneath that sunshine sign," explained the witch.

"This is ridiculous!" snorted Mr Fish, beginning to get rather cross. "There's no one there at all."

But the witch could clearly see Lady Fox-Custard's garden. The mayor had just arrived. There was a little table on the lawn, set out with scones and cream cakes. Lady Fox-Custard was dressed in her best dress – the one with poppies growing all over it, and she was pouring out the tea. She started to tell the mayor that she wanted his help to close down that ghastly café at the other end of town. The mayor looked hot and bothered.

"I thought it seemed rather a jolly sort of place," he muttered.

"JOLLY!" boomed Lady Fox-Custard. "It's crawl-ing with beetles. Goodness knows what germs are lurking in there. And the children should not be allowed to . . ."

At that moment, the witch at the BBC was

complaining. "You've got that sign all wrong, Mr Cod. It shouldn't be sunny. It should be raining and thunderin' and lightning."

And she changed the weather at once.

Immediately, a terrible downpour of rain came over Lady Fox-Custard's garden. The wind blew away all the cakes, and a fork of lightning struck the teapot.

"My goodness me!" gasped the mayor, and dashed off home, not waiting to hear what Lady Fox-Custard was in the middle of telling him.

When the witch arrived home, she started boasting madly.

"I've been on the telly, George," she hooted. "Did you see me? I could be a big star y'know. You should've seen Mr Kipper's face when I changed the weather!"

George went on nibbling the sideboard and took no notice. The witch leapt to the phone and rang Lady Fox-Custard.

"Did you like the weather this afternoon, Your Sunken-Ship?" she wheezed.

"Who is this?" roared Lady Fox-Custard, holding the phone at arm's length.

"It's Mr Jellied Eel," said the witch. "I'm in charge of bad weather."

And she put the phone down, cackling at her own wit.

All that week, the children worked happily in the witch's house. They painted ping pong balls different colours for the bingo game, and Sally and Angelica drew the cards and printed numbers on to them.

"I love this club," warbled Angelica. "I think I'll make a tiddlywink game as well."

"Tiddle away," said the witch. "I've got to write a letter to the mayor." She wrote,

Deer Mistur Mair,
There is a bingo game at
Valdeenees caffy tomorro
Plees cum and bring orl yor
frends Sined- The Witches Holiday Club
x x x

"The spelling's a bit funny," said Jimmy.

"Not as funny as that ping pong ball you've just painted," said the witch, squashing it with her foot.

And off she went to post the letter.

"By gum!" said the mayor. "Bingo, eh?"

He hoped there would be chocolate ice cream.

Valdini and Maria stayed up all night, polishing the café, stirring the spaghetti, and making lots of extra ice cream. In the morning, everything was ready. The witch and the children came and set up the bingo game. The witch sat at the door to take the money, and Angelica peeped down the road to see if anyone was coming.

"I can see thousands of people!" she squeaked.

Several people wandered into the café and looked around, admiringly. And then some more, and then some more again, and soon Valdini's was very full. Constable Scuff arrived and sat in a corner with his notebook. And then the mayor appeared.

"By Jove!" he said. "This looks wonderful. Just wonderful!"

"Have an ice cream, Your Warship," said the witch. "Never mind the queue."

By now, the café was so full, there was hardly room to move. The bingo game was making lots of money, and Maria was having to cook loads of extra spaghetti. Sally and Constable Scuff looked at one another and scowled.

"I wonder when the witch is going to hand over the stolen money?" Sally whispered.

"I'll have another of those delicious ice creams," the mayor was saying, pointing at the chocolate ices.

At that moment, Lady Fox-Custard peered through the window. She was deeply shocked to see the mayor, not only in the café, but actually enjoying himself. She beckoned to Constable Scuff.

"You're supposed to be keeping an eye on that monstrous woman, not having a good time!" she snarled.

"I am keeping an eye on her," grumbled Constable

Scuff, "and I'm not having a good time."

"Well get back in there," ordered Lady Fox-Custard. "I'm going to stay out here with me camera, and when that old biddy makes Valdini a rich man, I'm going to photograph her doing it, and that'll be EVIDENCE!"

The bingo went on, and the spaghetti and ice cream went on, and all the new customers went on, and Simon and the children thought it was the best day they had ever had.

Then Valdini opened his till and gasped.

"Mama mia!" he said. "Mrs Tatty has made me a rich man! Just like she promised."

"So *that's* what the witch meant!" groaned Constable Scuff.

"Oh dear!" wailed Sally, feeling very silly indeed.

Lady Fox-Custard's face went bright purple and wobbled like a dozen jellies.

"By Jove!" boomed the mayor, "this is the best food I've ever tasted. And this is the best café in the whole of the town. And you must come and do the food for the next Lord Mayor's banquet, Mr Valdini."

At this, Simon and the witch and everybody else in the Witch's Holiday Club cheered wildly.

"We've won!" cackled the witch to Simon.

Constable Scuff put away his little notebook and raced to get into the ice cream queue. He'd had quite enough of being bossed around by Lady Fox-Custard.